The Great Big DINOSAUR Treasury

Visit www.hmhbooks.com/freedownloads to download
and print accessories for your next dino party!

The Great Big DINOSAUR Treasury

TALES of ADVENTURE and DISCOVERY

Houghton Mifflin Harcourt

Boston New York

Dinosaurs captivate kids big and small . . . .

*T*he *Great Big Dinosaur Treasury* has enough prehistoric fun for the
entire family! Some dinosaur fans will be amazed to read in *Tadpole Rex*
that frogs lived at the time of the dinosaurs. Others may want to escape into
a fun-filled dinosaur fantasy aboard *Gus, the Dinosaur Bus.* And some dream
about how the world would look if dinosaurs walked among us, like Patrick
does in *Patrick's Dinosaurs.* No matter what kind of dinosaur story kids crave,
they'll find fun and exciting adventures in the pages of this book.

CONTENTS

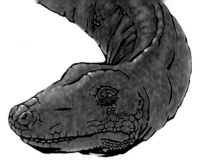

8   PATRICK'S DINOSAURS

41   CURIOUS GEORGE'S DINOSAUR DISCOVERY

67   IF THE DINOSAURS CAME BACK

95   TADPOLE REX

134   RIDIN' DINOS WITH BUCK BRONCO

171   GUS, THE DINOSAUR BUS

197   DINOSAILORS

229   GOOD NIGHT, DINOSAURS

260   MEET THE AUTHORS AND ILLUSTRATORS

PATRICK'S

By Carol Carrick

◊

Pictures by
Donald Carrick

DINOSAURS

P atrick and his brother, Hank, went to the zoo on Saturday. They stood outside a tall fence and watched the elephants.

"I'll bet that elephant is the biggest animal in the whole world," said Patrick.

"You think he's big," Hank said. "A brontosaurus was heavier than TEN elephants."

"Gosh!" said Patrick. If Hank said so, it must be true. Hank knew all about dinosaurs. He knew more about everything because he was older and went to school already.

Patrick squeezed his eyes half shut. What would a dinosaur that weighed as much as ten elephants look like? The brontosaurus he imagined turned and looked right at him.

"Did a brontosaurus eat people?" he asked nervously.

"Just plants," answered Hank.

Patrick's dinosaur started eating leaves from one of the trees.

They went to see the crocodiles next. Crocs were Patrick's favorite because he liked to scare himself.

"Those are shrimpy," said Hank. "In the days of dinosaurs, crocodiles grew three times that big."

"Wow!" said Patrick.

"Just their JAWS were twice as big as you are," added Hank.

Patrick imagined an enormous crocodile. It was three times bigger than the other crocs. It was so big that it wanted the whole pool for itself.

The other crocodiles were too slow getting out. So the enormous crocodile opened its jaws that were twice as big as Patrick and gobbled them all up.

Patrick backed away. "We didn't see the monkeys yet."

After they had seen the monkeys and the seals, Patrick and Hank went for a row on the zoo lake.

Patrick looked down into the deep green water. What was that dark shape next to their boat? "Did dinosaurs know how to swim?" he asked.

"Some did," answered Hank. "Diplodocus, the longest dinosaur, could stay under water like a submarine because its nose was on top of its head."

Patrick was afraid to move. Out of the corner of his eyes he saw the big thing swimming along next to them. It might rise and dump them over!

"WHAT'S THAT!" he cried. "We're going to bump into it!"

"No, dopey. That's just the shadow from our boat," Hank explained.

Patrick wasn't so sure. "Let's go home now," he said. "Rowing makes me tired."

When they got on the bus Patrick felt better, even though Hank was still showing off how much he knew about dinosaurs.

"A stegosaurus was bigger than one of those cars," Hank said. "But its brain was only the size of a walnut."

Patrick looked out the window. In his mind the lane of cars was a line of walnut-brained stegosauruses. The plates on their backs swayed like sails as they plodded along.

Hank reached up and rang the bell for the driver to stop. "A triceratops was tougher than a stegosaurus," he said. "It could even take on a tyrannosaurus."

The bus stopped at their corner. On the other side of the street Patrick thought he saw a triceratops waiting for the traffic light.

When Patrick and his brother climbed down from the bus, the hot dusty street became a prehistoric forest. Tropical birds screamed their warning. Too late. A dreadful tyrannosaurus crashed into the clearing.

Patrick held his breath as the triceratops lowered its huge head. Its horns pointed ahead like three enormous spears. When the traffic light changed, the triceratops charged.

"RUN!" Patrick yelled. He headed for their apartment building.

"What's the hurry?" called Hank.

Patrick didn't feel safe until the front door of the hall slammed shut. He wanted to look out his window, but first he had to ask Hank something.

"How big was a tyrannosaurus?"

"Big," said Hank.

"Up to the second floor, maybe?" asked Patrick.

"At least," Hank agreed.

"That's what I was afraid of," said Patrick.

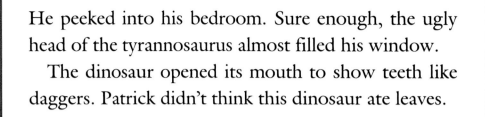

He peeked into his bedroom. Sure enough, the ugly head of the tyrannosaurus almost filled his window.

The dinosaur opened its mouth to show teeth like daggers. Patrick didn't think this dinosaur ate leaves.

"Are you SURE there are no more dinosaurs around?" he asked Hank.

"Positive. The dinosaurs have been gone for sixty million years."

Patrick gave a sigh of relief. And the dinosaur disappeared.

MARGRET & H. A. REY'S
Curious George's
Dinosaur Discovery

Written by Catherine Hapka

Illustrated in the style of H. A. Rey by Anna Grossnickle Hines

This is George.

He was a good little monkey and always very curious.

George loved to go places with his friend the man with the yellow hat. One of their favorite places to visit was the Dinosaur Museum.

"Today is a special day," George's friend said. "We are going to do something very interesting!"

George was curious. What could be more interesting than a trip to the Dinosaur Museum?

The man with the yellow hat led the way through the museum. George wanted to stop and look at the dinosaur bones. But his friend kept going, so George kept following.

Finally they walked right out the back door!

A van was waiting for them outside. "Climb in, George," said the man with the yellow hat.

George looked out the window as the van drove off. Where could they be going?

At last, the van reached a rocky quarry. Dozens of people were there. Some were digging with shovels. Others were using pickaxes or other kinds of tools.

"Surprise!" George's friend said. "We're going to help the museum scientists dig for dinosaur bones!"

George was curious. Were there really dinosaurs buried in the quarry? He ran over for a better look. "Hello," said a friendly scientist. "Are you here to help with the dig?"

George watched the scientist work. She dug up some dirt and put it into her sifting pan.

It took a long time to sift it. And in the end — no dinosaur bones!

"Oh, well," she said. "Time to try again!"

But the next pan was empty, too. So was the next one. And the one after that.

George yawned. So far digging for dinosaurs was not as exciting as he'd expected.

George was curious. Could he help to find dinosaur bones?

He found a spare shovel lying nearby. He dug and dug.
But he didn't find any dinosaurs.

When he climbed out of his hole, George spotted another scientist. He was dusting something with a small brush.

"Oh, well," the scientist said. "It's not a bone. Just a rock."

George wanted to help. He picked up a brush and went to work.

But it turns out that monkeys are not very good at dusting!

As he hurried away from the cloud of dust, George bumped
into a wheelbarrow. Maybe there were dinosaur bones in it!

He climbed up to look inside. But the wheelbarrow was
awfully tippy . . .

CRASH!

George, the wheelbarrow, and a whole lot of dirt went flying.
"Hey!" someone cried. "What's that monkey doing?"

George scampered away, straight up the cliff. Monkeys are good at climbing, so George kept going — higher and higher.

When he got to the top, he accidentally knocked a stone over the edge.

That stone hit another stone . . .

which hit another stone . . .

and another . . .

Oh, no! It was a rockslide!

The man with the yellow hat
called for George to come down.
George wanted to climb down,
but he was afraid the scientists
would be angry with him.

But the scientists didn't
look angry.

"Look!" one cried,
pointing. "Look what that
monkey just uncovered!"

George could hardly believe what he saw. Dinosaur bones!

After that, the dinosaur dig was even more fun. George helped the scientists dig . . .

and sift . . .

and dust . . .

and take photographs of
the bones he had found.

And the next time he and the man with the yellow hat visited the Dinosaur Museum, George got to see HIS dinosaur on display!

For Eric and especially for Glenn,
who wished the dinosaurs would come back

If the dinosaurs came back

Written and illustrated by
Bernard Most

I like dinosaurs.
I think about them all the time.
I read about them.
I talk about them.
Oh, how I wish the dinosaurs
could come back!

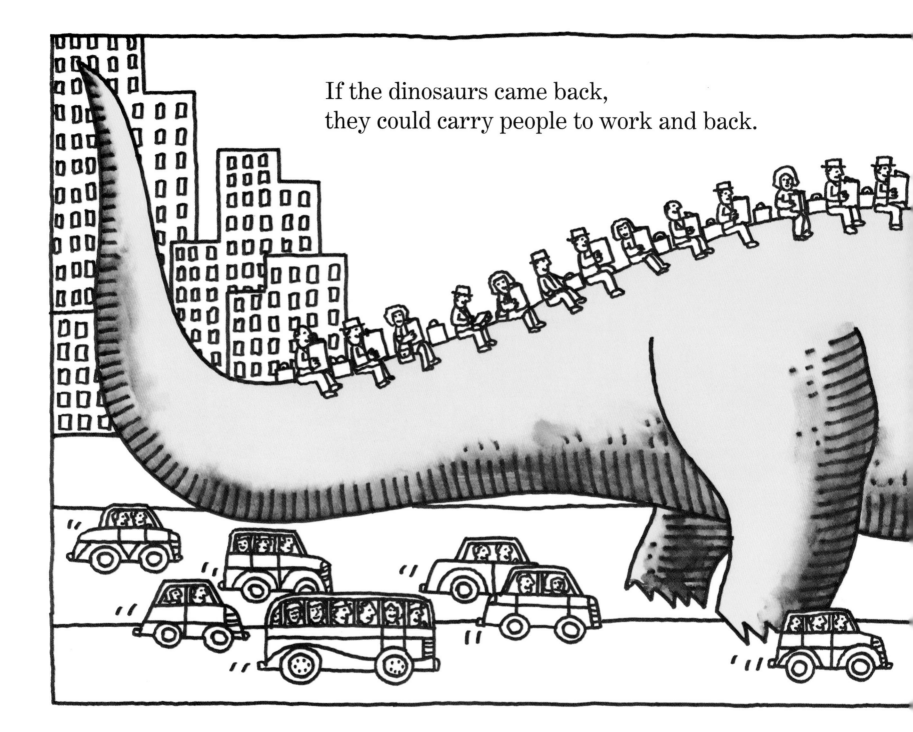

If the dinosaurs came back,
they could carry people to work and back.

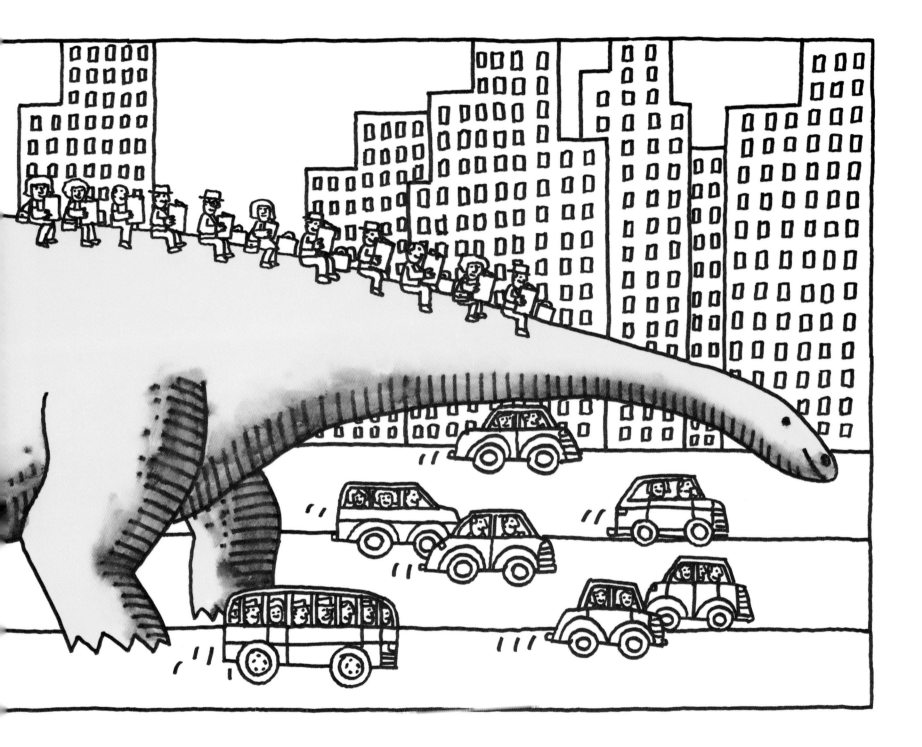

If the dinosaurs came back,
we wouldn't need
any more lawn mowers.

If the dinosaurs came back, house painters wouldn't need any more ladders.

If the dinosaurs came back,
they would scare away robbers.

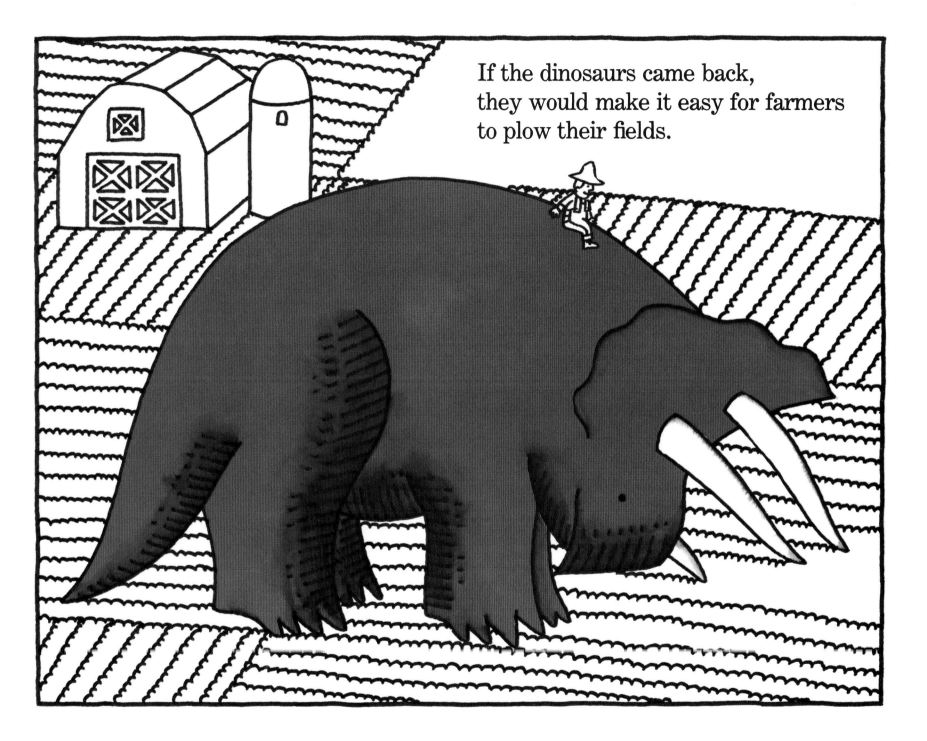

If the dinosaurs came back,
they would make it easy for farmers
to plow their fields.

If the dinosaurs came back,
they could help lumberjacks chop down trees.

If the dinosaurs came back,
they could help firefighters
put out fires.

If the dinosaurs came back,
they could help build
big skyscrapers.

If the dinosaurs came back,
they would make great ski slopes.

If the dinosaurs came back,
they could take swimmers
on rides at the beach.

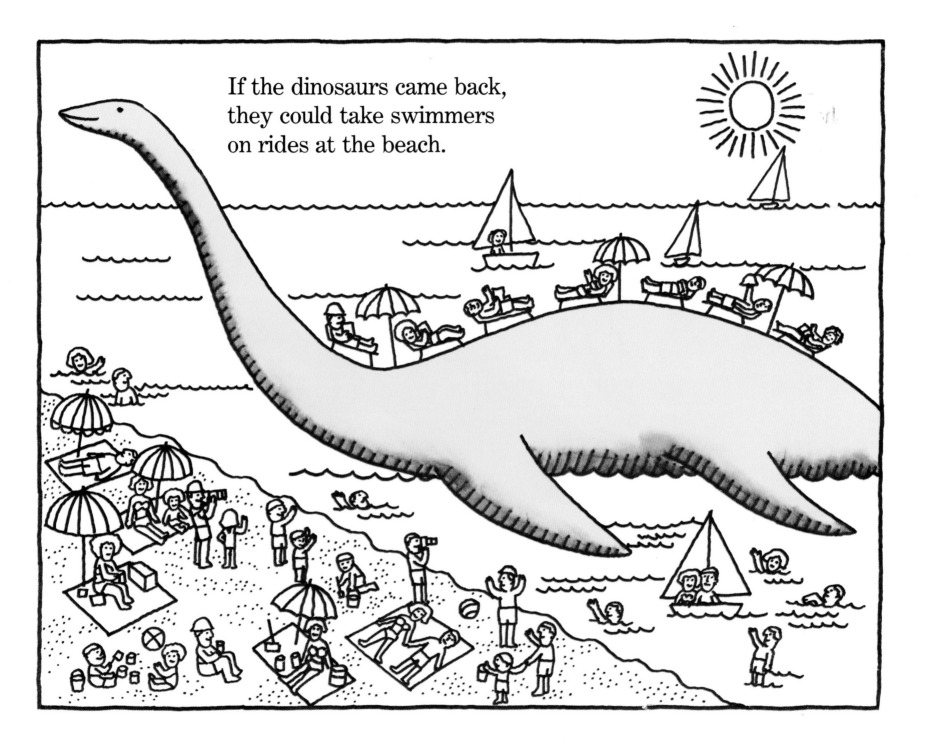

If the dinosaurs came back,
they could rescue kites
stuck in very tall trees.

If the dinosaurs came back, mountain climbers would have new mountains to climb.

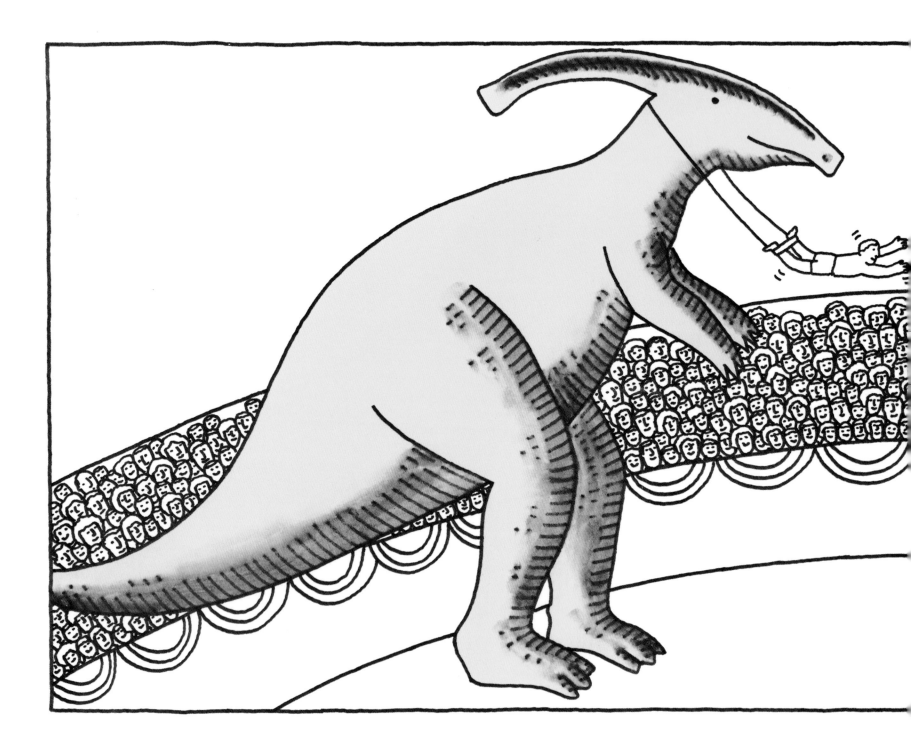

If the dinosaurs came back,
they could be a big help at the circus.

If the dinosaurs came back,
they could help librarians get books
from the top shelf.

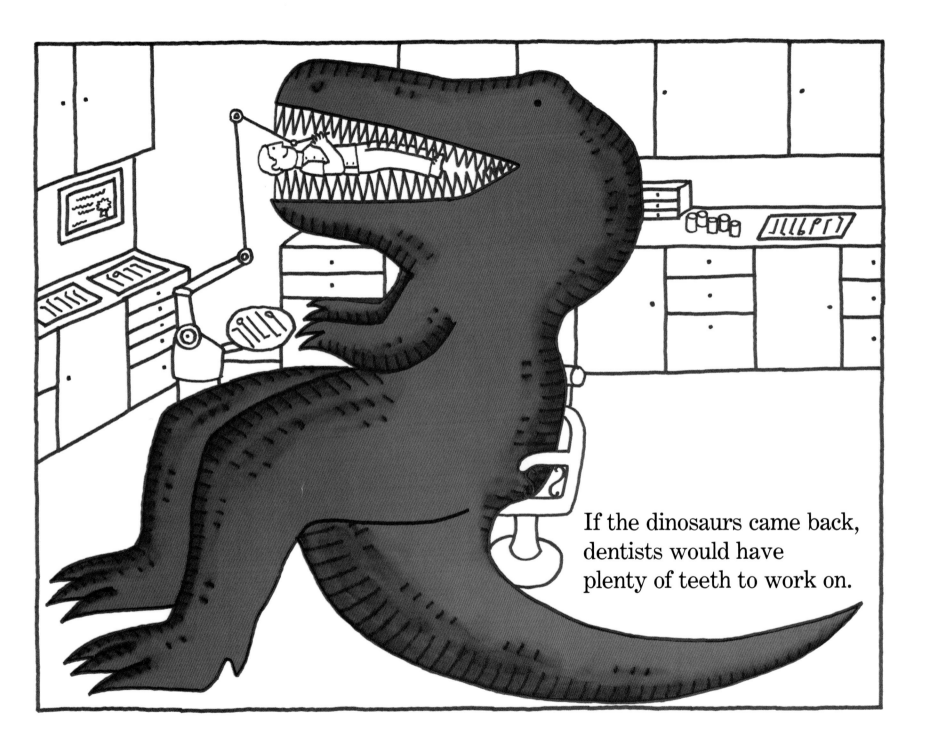

If the dinosaurs came back, dentists would have plenty of teeth to work on.

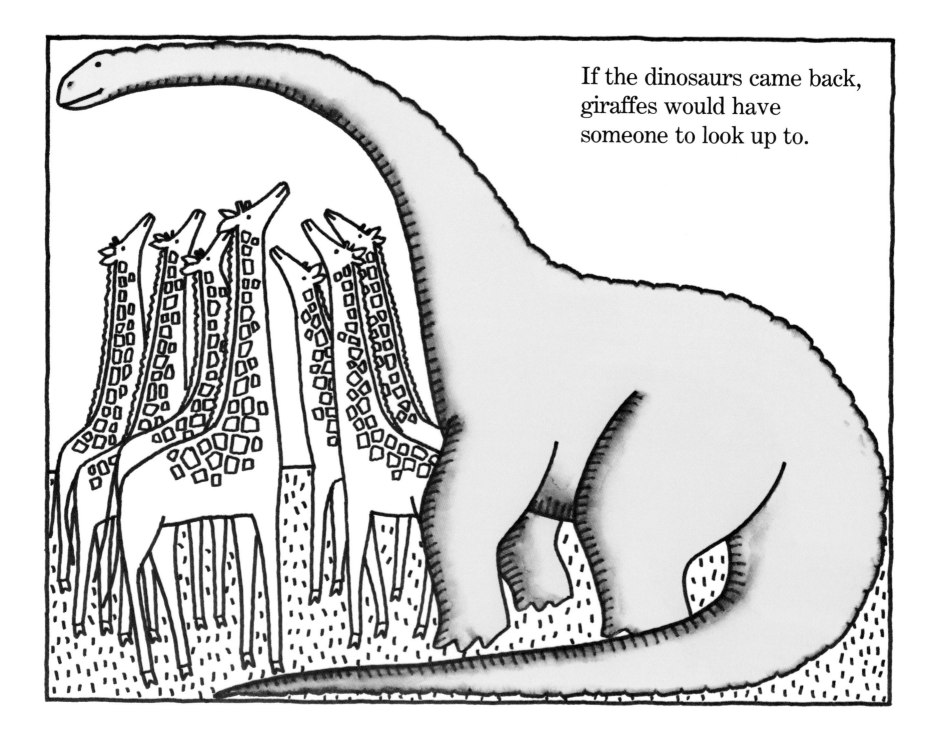

If the dinosaurs came back, giraffes would have someone to look up to.

If the dinosaurs came back,
they could push away rain clouds
so the sun would always shine.

But best of all...if the dinosaurs came back,
they would make great
pets for people who love dinosaurs.

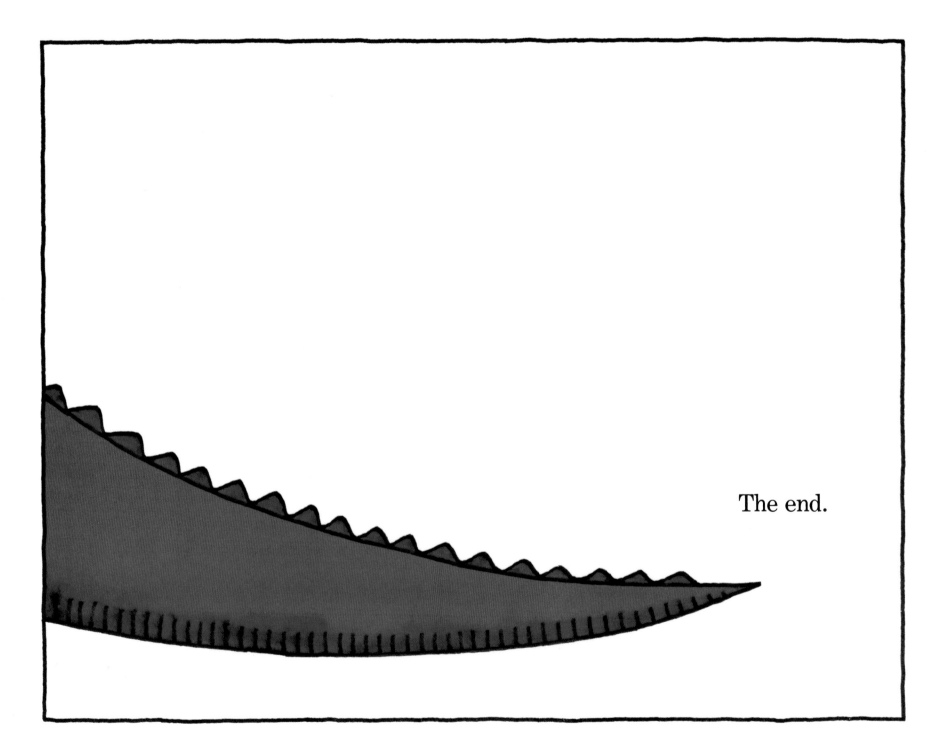

The end.

If the dinosaurs came back, this is what you would call them:

Diplodocus Corythosaurus Triceratops Apatosaurus Dimetrodon*

Ornithomimus

Tyrannosaurus Iguanodon Plateosaurus Allosaurus Parasaurolophus Edmontosaurus

Plesiosaurus* Megalosaurus Brachiosaurus Stegosaurus Hypselosaurus

Ceratosaurus Coelophysis Scelidosaurus Camptosaurus Protoceratops Centrosaurus

* Scientists do not consider Dimetrodon and Plesiosaurus to be dinosaurs, but they were prehistoric creatures.

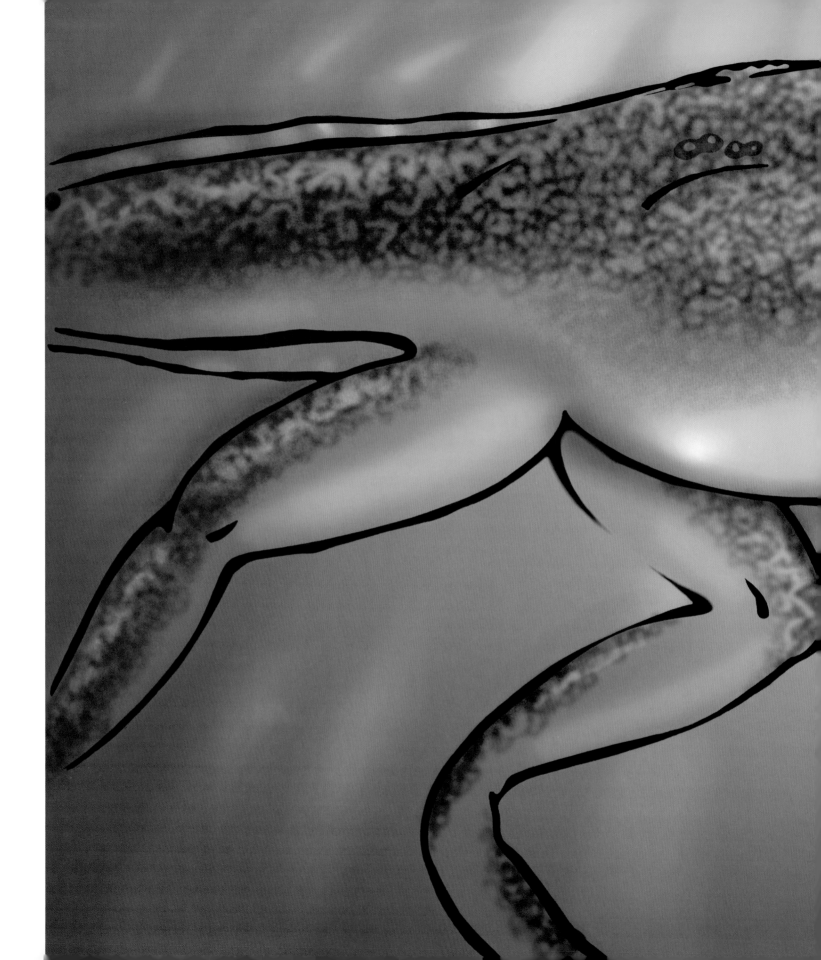

Tadpole REX

BY
KURT CYRUS

Deep in the goop of a long-ago swamp,
a whopping big dinosaur went for a stomp.

Stomp! went the dinosaur. **Squish!** went the goop.
Up came the bubbles—
Bloop.
Bloop.
Bloop.

Swish went the horsetails, tattered and torn.
Then water rushed in . . .

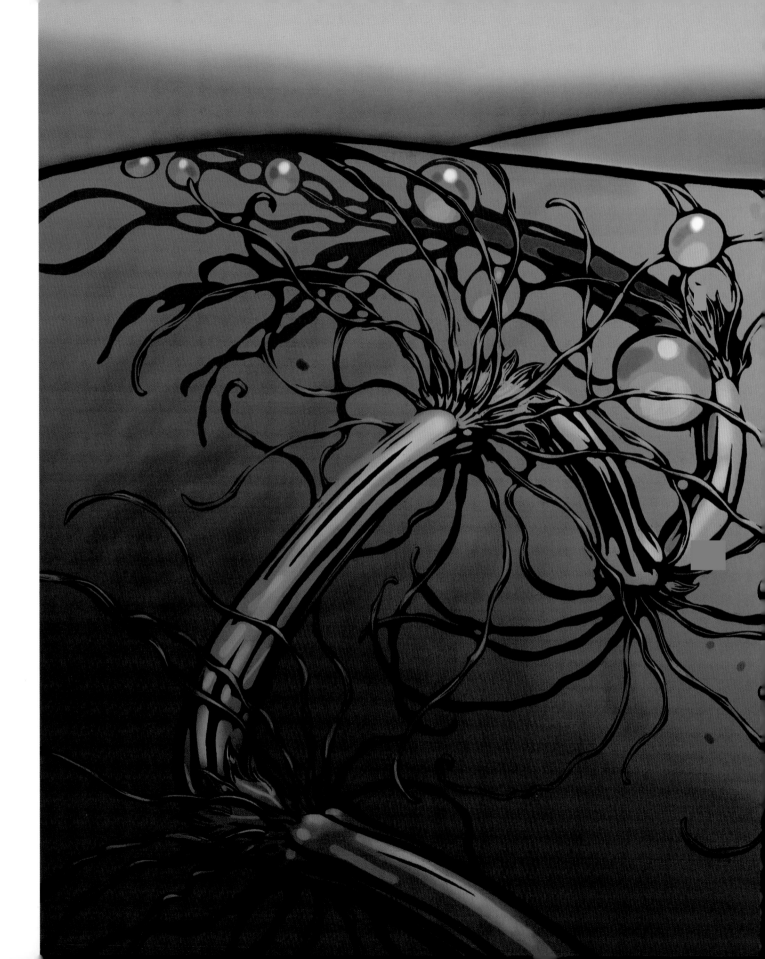

. . . and a puddle was born.

One little polliwog swirled in the soup,

bouncing off bubbles—

Bloop.

Bloop.

Bloop.

Barely a dot. Scarcely a speck.

A head with a tail. No legs. No neck.

A mouth and a belly, and that's about all.

Tadpole Rex was remarkably small.

Primeval puddles were desperate places
of ambush and panic and life-or-death chases.

Stuck in a footprint with nowhere to go,
surrounded by giants, Rex lay low.
Mud was his camouflage. Mud was his friend.
But Rex wouldn't wallow in mud in the end. . . .

For somewhere inside him, deep in his core,
there slumbered an inner tyrannosaur.
A Rex who was fearless, with fire in his blood—

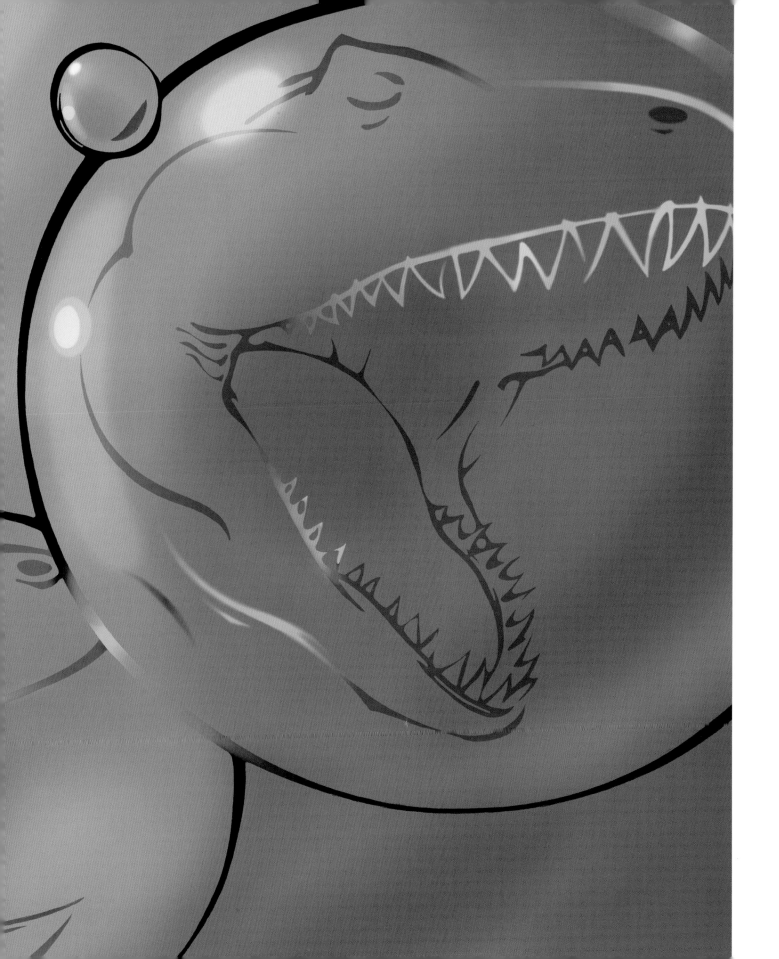

Splash! went a hunter.
Rex hit the mud.

But soon Rex grew,
as tadpoles do.

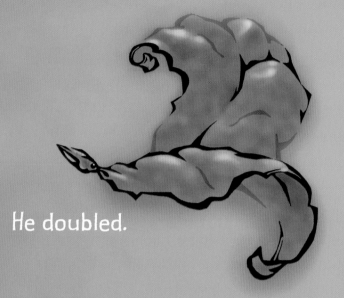

He doubled.

He tripled.

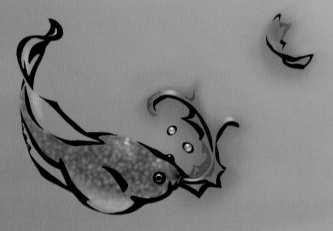

He grew by four.

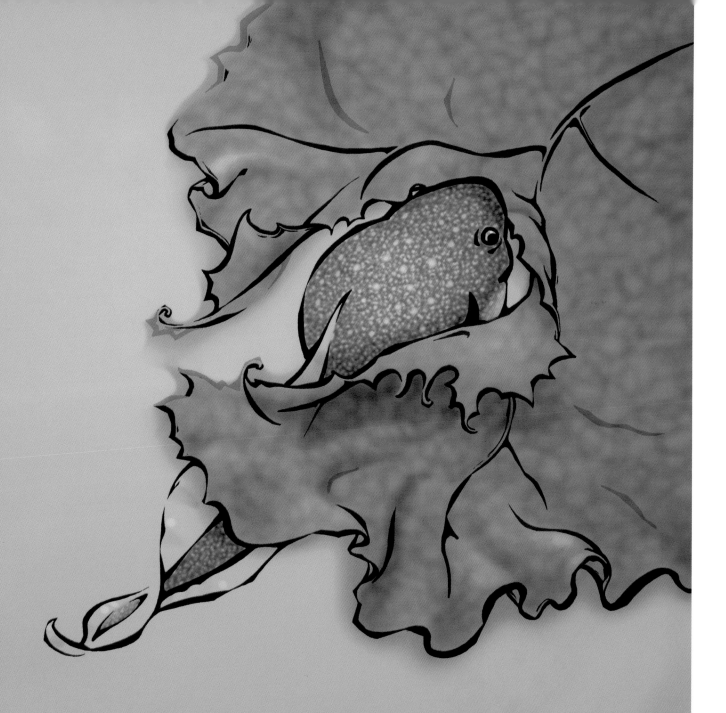

He ate like a hungry tyrannosaur.
And then . . .

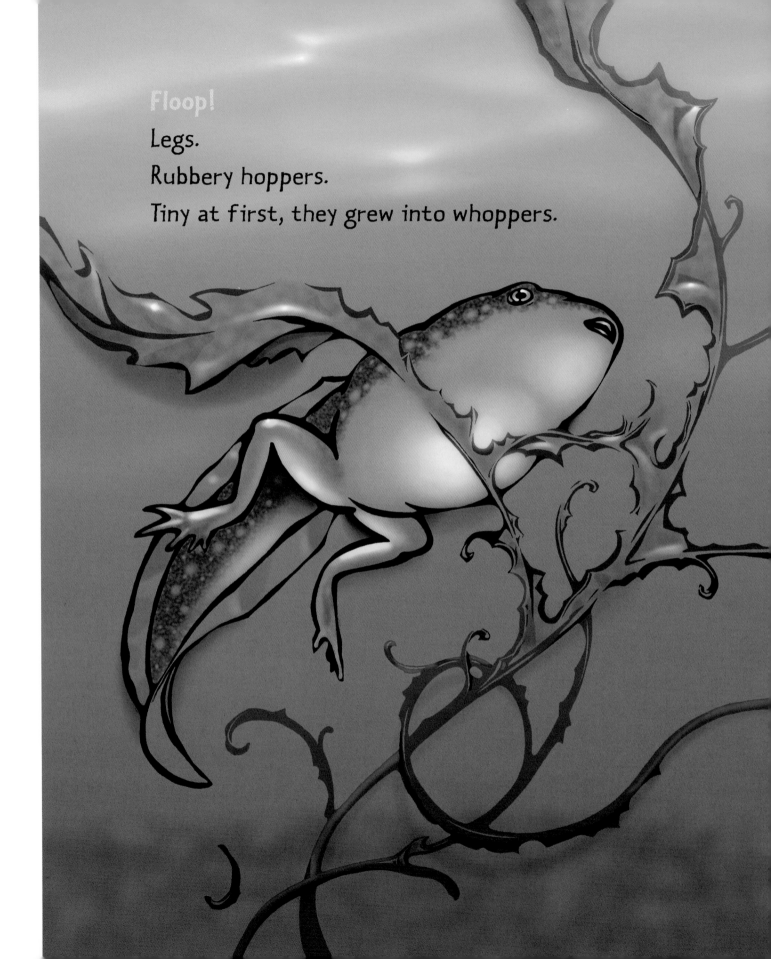

Floop!

Legs.

Rubbery hoppers.

Tiny at first, they grew into whoppers.

Fleep!

Arms.

Supple and bendable.

Not very strong, but still, dependable.

Patience and time. That's all it took.

Suddenly Rex had a whole new look.

Rex didn't hide in the goop anymore.
Out came his inner tyrannosaur!

Inflating his throat and lifting his head,
Rex gave a roar—

Ribbet! he said.

Lumbering duckbills were taken aback
to see an amphibian on the attack.

Alamosauruses craned their necks
to get a good look at Tadpole Rex.

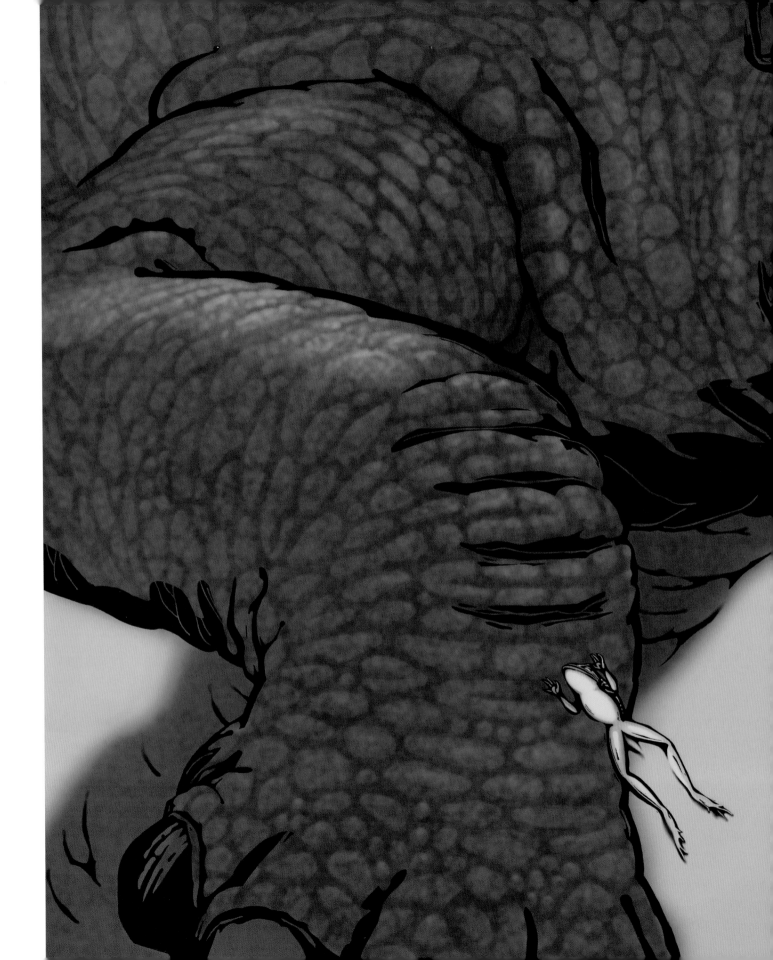

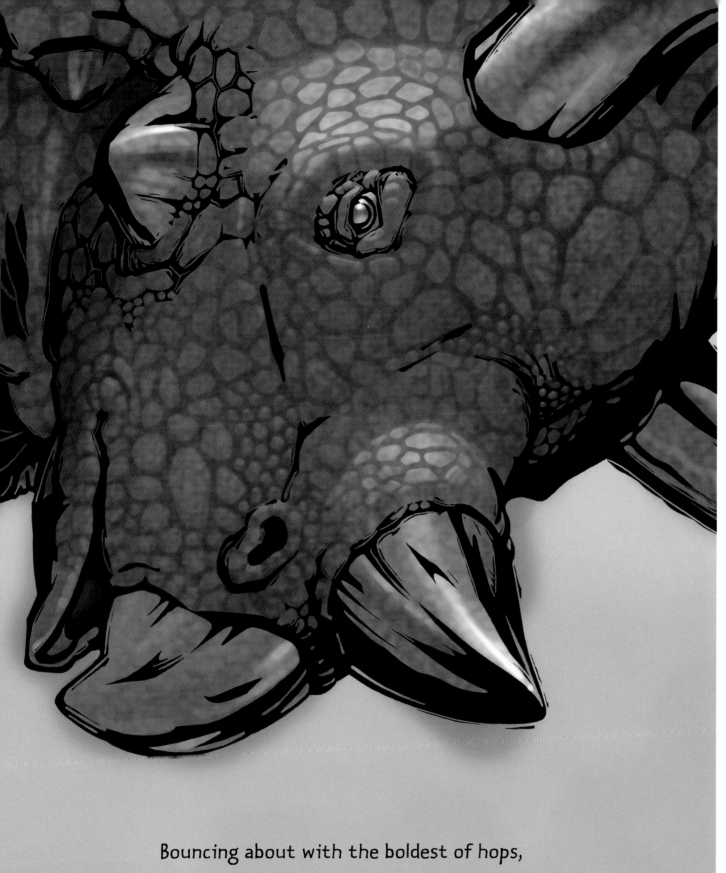

Bouncing about with the boldest of hops,
Rex nearly tripped a triceratops.

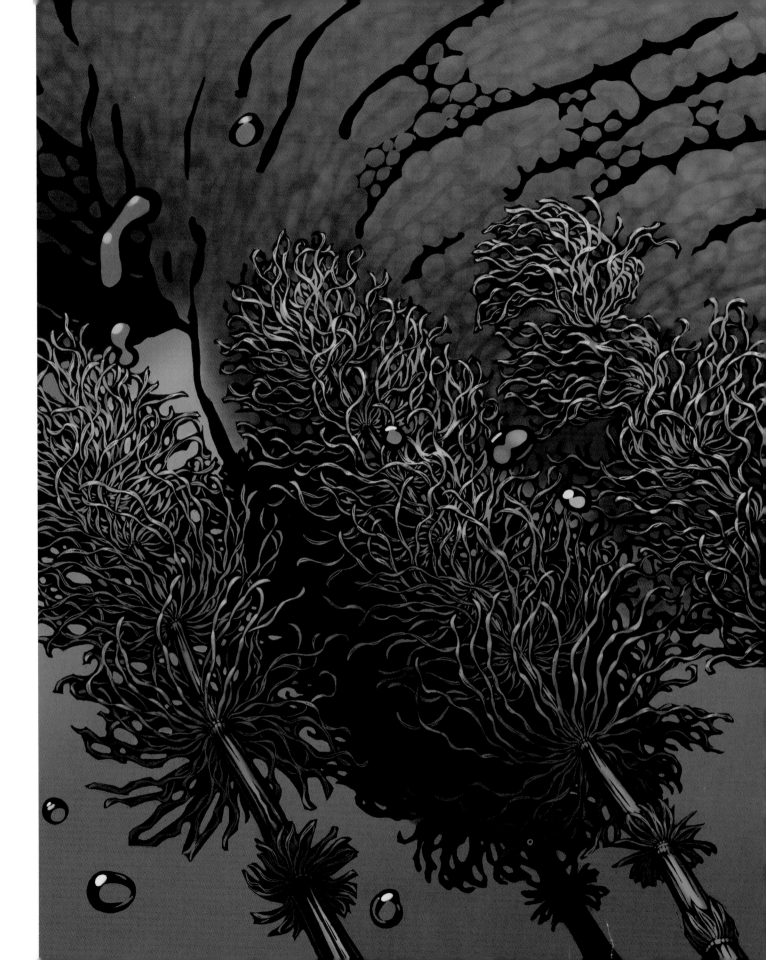

Stomp! went the dinosaur.
Squish! went the goop.
Ribbet! went Rex.
Bloop.
Bloop.
Bloop.

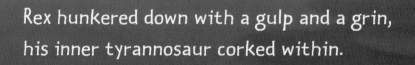

Rex hunkered down with a gulp and a grin,
his inner tyrannosaur corked within.

Two blinking eyes. That's all he let show,
watching the dinosaurs come and go.

Gone are the dinosaurs. Gone are the stompers,
the rippers, the roarers, the bone-crunching chompers.
Gone are the dinosaurs, swept away. . . .

But hoppers and croakers are here to stay.

Tree frogs and bullfrogs and little spring peepers,
sure-footed climbers and long-distance leapers.
Frogs of all fashions continue to huddle
around any suitable freshwater puddle.

And somewhere inside,
deep in their core,
they *all* have an inner
tyrannosaur.

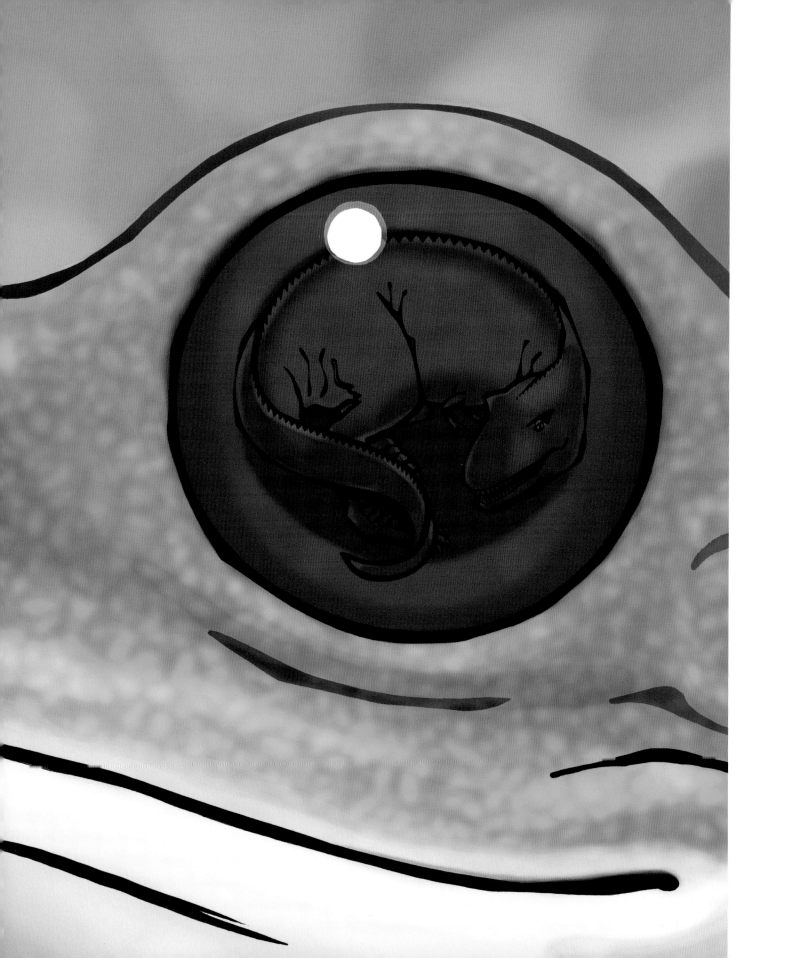

A Note from the Author

Does a tadpole really have an inner tyrannosaur? Yes . . . in a way.
When a tadpole becomes a frog, it does more than grow limbs and lose its tail.
Unseen changes take place inside as well. Gills are replaced by lungs so the frog can
live on land. At the same time, its digestive system transforms. The plant-eating
tadpole becomes a meat-eating frog. When Rex emerges from his puddle in this
story, he is hungry for live prey—just like a tyrannosaur.

Frogs really did live alongside tyrannosaurs and triceratops. In fact, frogs existed
100 million years *before* these particular dinosaurs evolved. Fossils show that some
prehistoric frogs had short legs, while others had long. Some had wide heads, others
narrow. And many, like Rex, had well-developed teeth. Frogs came in all shapes and
sizes, just as they do today.

After 200 million years on Earth, frogs now find their world changing rapidly.
New challenges—pollution, habitat loss, climate change—are taking a severe toll.
As scientists search for solutions to these problems, we can hope that hoppers and
croakers will be around to enrich ecosystems for many more millions of years.

Many thanks to Linnea

Ridin' Dinos with Buck Bronco

with

Buck Bronco

As told to **George McClements**

Fer my posse:

Rachel, Samuel, and Matthew

Howdy, kids! The name is

Buck Br

onco,

and I'm here to teach y'all everything
you need to know 'bout ridin' dinosaurs,
includin' how I met these curious critters.

It all started when I brought home some loco-lookin' eggs that I found in my back field.

I was surely surprised when they began to hatch.

I had to do some quick-time learnin'.

And today I'm called
a leadin' authority on dinosaurs.

Now let's stop all
this tongue waggin'
and git to ridin'!

Choosin' Yer Mount

First, you'll need to pick out a dino from my Mesozoic Ranch. I have three different stables to choose from.

Biped=2 legs

You'll have to decide between the speed of a biped or the comfort of a quadruped.

Quadruped=4 legs

You vegetarians out there may want to choose an herbivore over a steak-chompin' carnivore.

Dinosaurs come in
so many shapes and sizes,
I'm sure you'll find one
to match yer personality.

Saddlin' Yer Dino

Next, unless ya got glue in yer britches, we'll need to tack up!

Take a look at what we got:

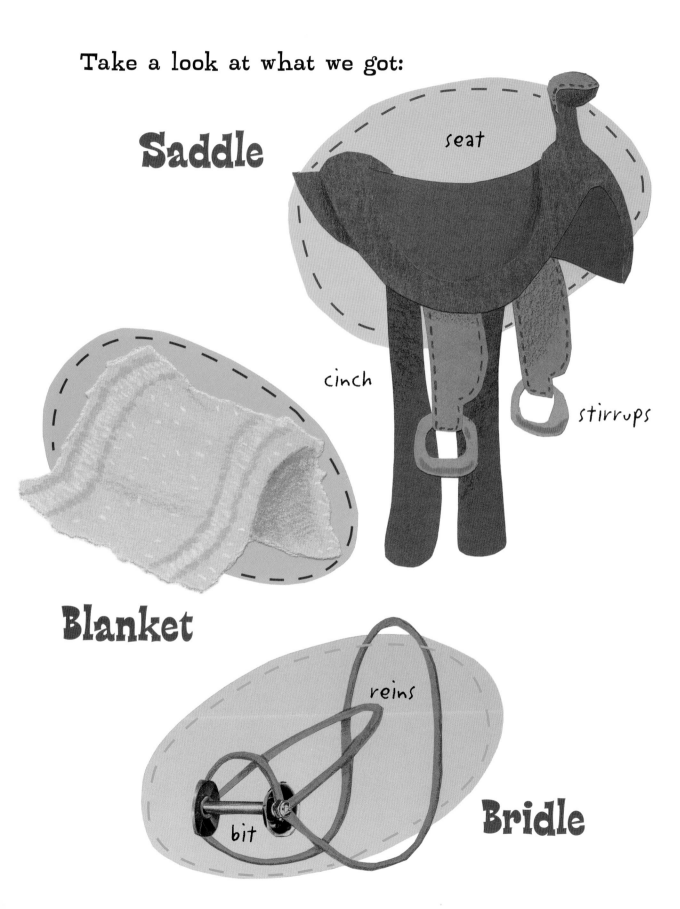

Saddle

seat

cinch

stirrups

Blanket

Bridle

reins

bit

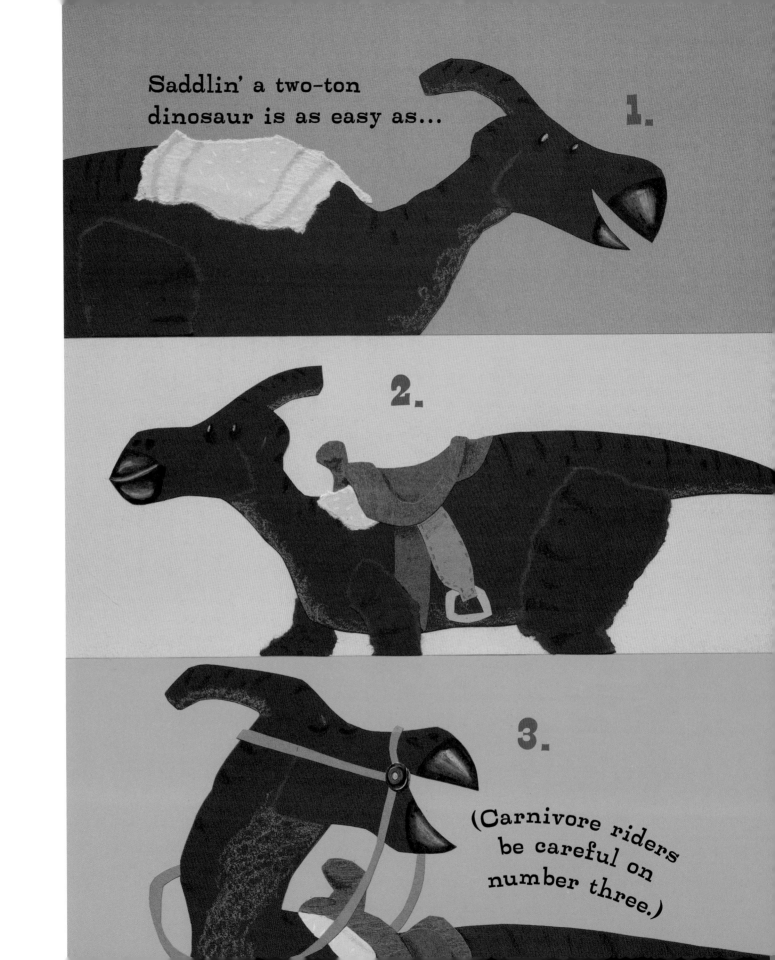

Saddlin' a two-ton dinosaur is as easy as...

1.

2.

3.

(Carnivore riders be careful on number three.)

A little creativity helps with the big boys.

Diplodocus = 88 feet long

I like to use somethin' called the polecat hop to git into my saddle.

First, you line up yer seat...

then you kick up some dust...

grab some air...

...and two somersaults later, yer sittin' pretty.

A kentrosaurus may present some special problems, so I suggest usin' a ladder.

Now that we're strapped in, let's git movin'! Luckily, I got these handy talkin' boards to help us along.

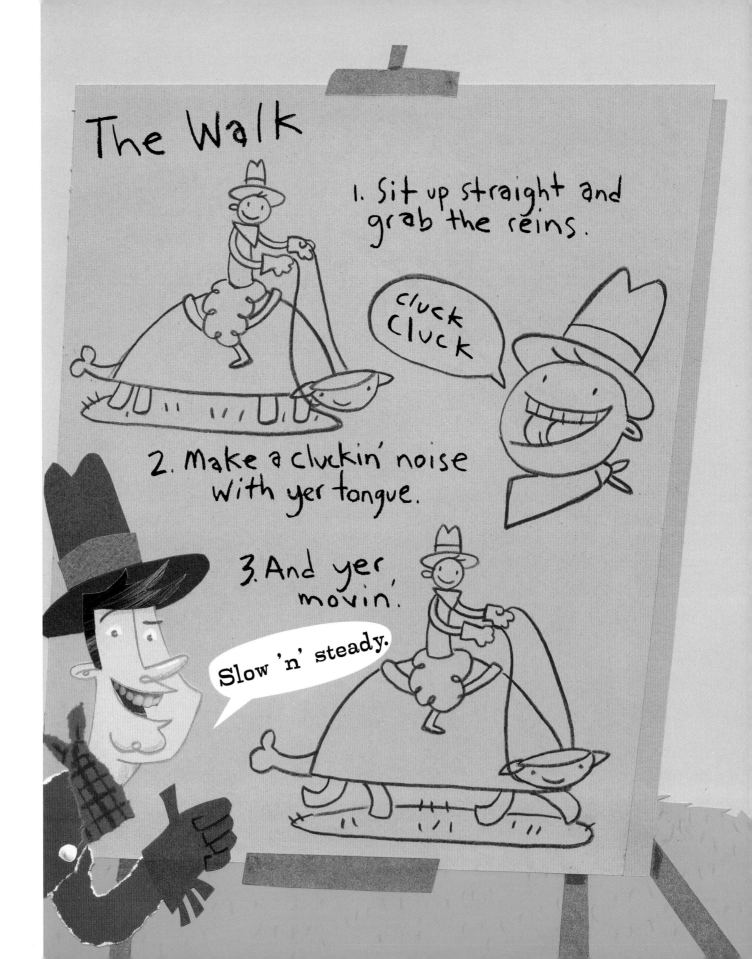

The Trot

This should be a nice, gentle acceleration.

(Unless you're ridin' a gallimimus, capable of speeds over twenty-five miles an hour!)

The Jump
1. Gently squeeze yer heels.
2. Git yer dino to scrunch up his legs.
3. And push off into the wild blue yonder.
Now that's fancy!

After the Ride

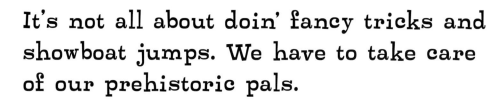

It's not all about doin' fancy tricks and showboat jumps. We have to take care of our prehistoric pals.

Yer dinosaur will be powerful thirsty after all that runnin' around. So make certain he gits his fill of water.

Rock

Stick

Puppy

woof!

Always check yer dino's
feet fer any foreign objects.

You may need some help
with a deinonychus.
That five-inch claw
can pack a wallop!

These critters can sure work up an appetite.
Here's a few suggestions fer suppertime:

Herbivores

leaves

nuts and berries

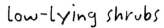

low-lying shrubs

Carnivores

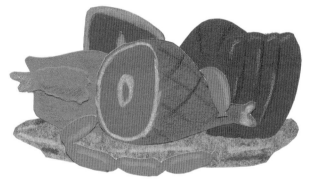

meat

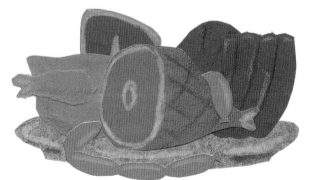

meat

meat

At the End of the Day

Compsognathus=40 inches

Size 12½

Don't forget to give yer dino a comfy place to bed down.

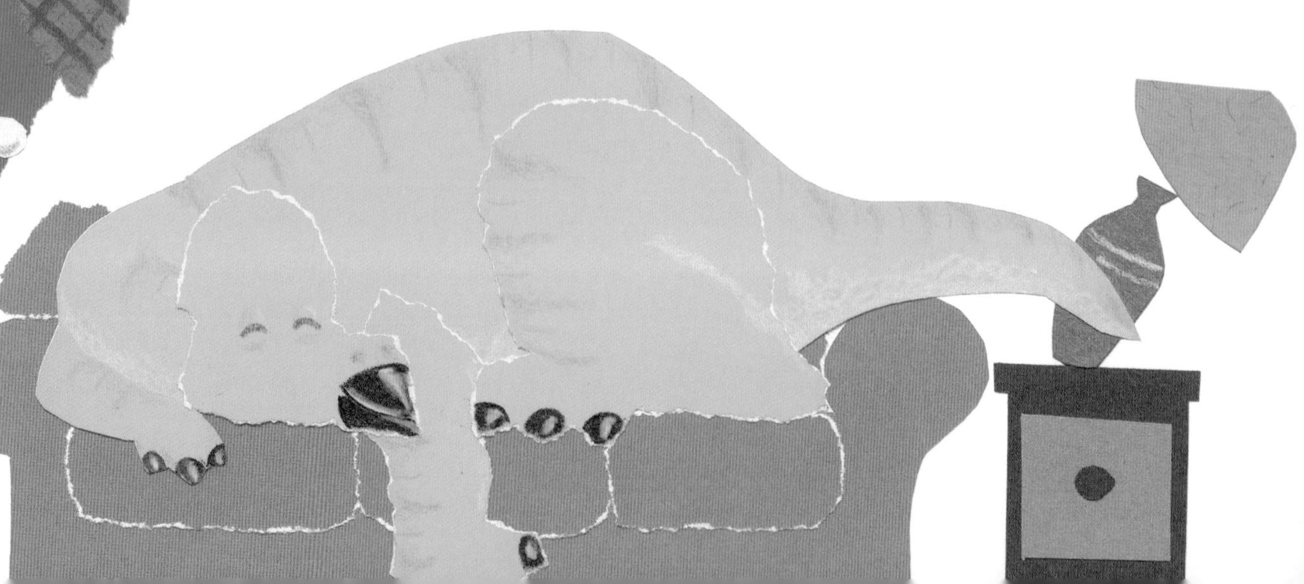

I find it best to let the big guys pick their own spots.

Spinosaurus=40 feet

HATCHERY

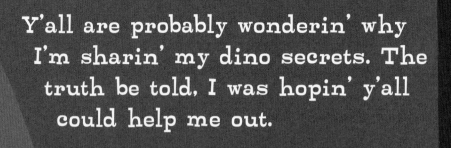

Y'all are probably wonderin' why I'm sharin' my dino secrets. The truth be told, I was hopin' y'all could help me out.

Now that yer dinosaur experts...

Would you mind if
I sent you a couple
of eggs?

Gus, the Dinosaur Bus

Written by Julia Liu
Illustrated by Bei Lynn

In the city, children are going to school.
Some walk.
Some ride in a car.
Some take a yellow bus.
But the lucky children of one school ride something different.

Gus, the dinosaur bus!

Every morning, Gus stomps down the streets to pick up his passengers. Nobody sleeps late or pretends to be sick. They can't wait for Gus to arrive.

Who needs a bus stop when you have a dinosaur bus? Gus comes right to the door. The children who live in apartments don't even need to walk downstairs. They hop out their windows and slide down to their seats.

Wheee!

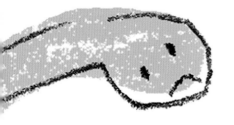

Riding a dinosaur bus means never stopping for gas or being stuck in traffic.

"Honk! Honk! Dinosaur coming through!" the people shout.

Gus is careful not to step on any cars. But still, his big feet are a worry, so . . .

The city makes a new road just for Gus.

Along his route, people leave him snacks. Like two tons of french fries.

Road crews repair the dino-size potholes that Gus accidentally leaves behind.

Everyone at school loves Gus.

He helps them reach high places . . . and a supersaurus makes a good umbrella.

But life is not perfect for a dinosaur bus.

Gus is so tall that he often gets tangled in telephone lines. He bumps his head on overpasses. He has been known to knock down a traffic light or two.

When you're as wide as a tennis court, you can cause traffic jams for miles and miles. And it's not easy to cross bridges when you weigh as much as five elephants.

Careful, Gus!

Gus's tail is trouble too. Sometimes when he turns corners, he knocks down a house roof. Lately, the school is getting more and more complaints. Police officers keep dropping off tickets. The bills to fix the things Gus has broken are piling up.

"Gus is causing a BIG fuss!" says the principal. "What am I going to do?"

The principal has no choice. He pulls Gus off the road. Gus is so sad that he hides in the gym and cries and cries. Just one of Gus's tears could fill a bathtub. Each one falls to the ground with a

SPLAT!

The children crowd into the gym to cheer him up.

"Don't worry," they say, hugging their big green friend. "We will keep you company."

Gus is beginning to feel better. But — oh, no! The smallest girl has lost hold of his neck and is sliding down it.

"Whoa!" she cries . . .

"Hey!" she shouts. "Where did this pool come from?"

"Look, Gus!" says the teacher. "You've made a swimming pool with your tears."

The children cheer. "Hooray! Gus can play with us again!"
And they slide into their new pool.

Now Gus is no longer a dinosaur bus.
He's Gus, the dinosaur slide!
And swing.
And playground.

Every day, the children visit him to swim, slide, swing, and climb.
Maybe one day you can visit Gus too. But you'll have to be patient.

The line is long.

DINOSAILORS

DEB LUND

Illustrated by

HOWARD FINE

For Uncle Vern and the Shifty Sailors
—D.L.

For Bo and Rhino
—H.F.

Dinosailors at the slip
Cry out, "Ahoy!" and board their ship.
They swab the deck, stow dinogear,
Ignoring clouds that linger near.

They're hale and hearty—dinotough!
They talk of salty sailing stuff:
Blocks and winches, dinocleats,
Shackles, tacking, trimming sheets.

Dinosailors choose a course,
Raise anchor using dinoforce.
They haul on lines, hoist dinosails,
And scale the rigging with their tails.

Dinosingers sing a song,
Tenors, basses booming strong:
"Heave ho! Heave ho! This life's for me,
Dinosailing on the sea!"

Dinosailors have a ball,
Until their vessel hits a squall.
The water tosses all around.
Their dinofeet miss solid ground.

They dinosault like Ping-Pong balls,
Bumping dinorumps and walls.
Dinoswingers hang from sails.
They mash the mast and ram the rails.

Dinodiners in the galley
Do not stop to dillydally.
Grabbing grub, they gobble up,
Gripping dinofork and cup.

Their dinotummies slosh and churn.
They groan with every twist and turn.
Their paling faces dinofrown.
"Heave ho!" they cry. "It won't stay down!"

Dinosailors need a break.
They shiver, ache, and dinoshake.
Though winds die down to just a breeze,
They still have wobbly dinoknees.

The woozy dinos moan and weep.
The day's been long—they need some sleep.
In dinojammies at the head,
They brush and floss, then climb in bed.

When they awake, they cry, "No more!"
"We're sick of decks—we want a floor!"

Dinowhiners reach the land
And stagger off, so glad to stand.

Dinosailors sell that boat.
They'd rather dinostroll than float.
They go back home to those they miss,
To cuddle, hug, and dinokiss.

This dinolife is calm and slow,
For dinos who were on the go.
Once more they hear adventure's cry,
So dinotravelers say good-bye.

No more a seasick dinobunch,
They find a way to keep their lunch.
In harmony, they join the chord . . .

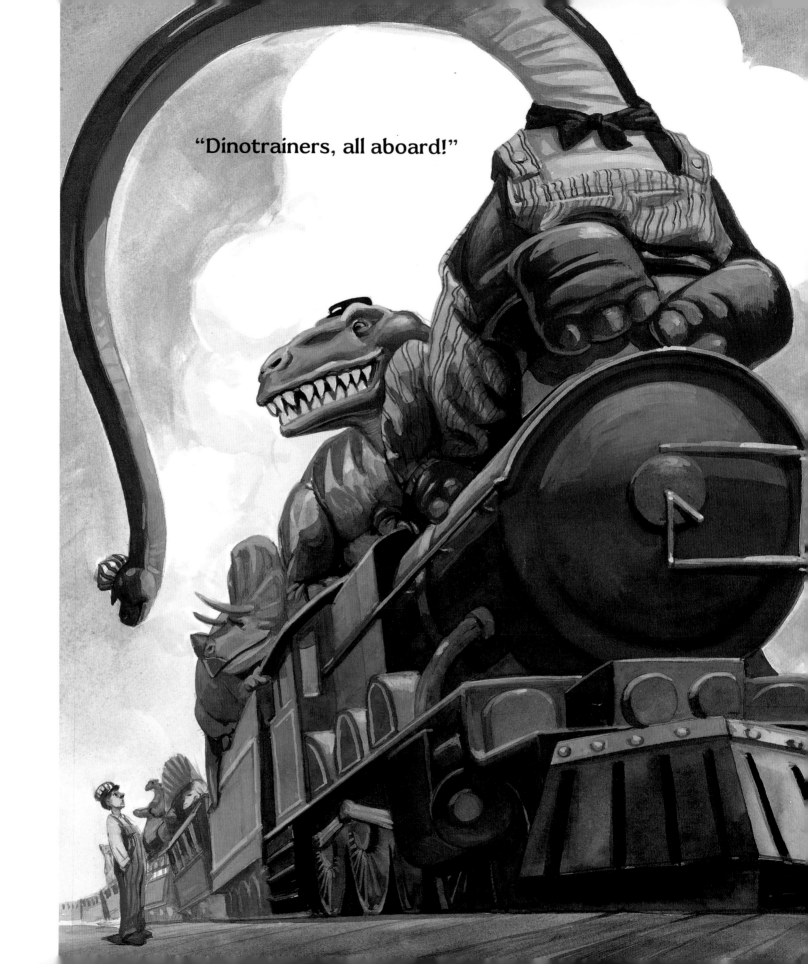

"Dinotrainers, all aboard!"

226

*GOOD *NIGHT*
DINOSAURS

BY JUDY SIERRA
ILLUSTRATED BY VICTORIA CHESS

For Kosta Horaites
—J.S.

* ＊ ✳ ＊ *

For Phoebe, with love
—V.C.

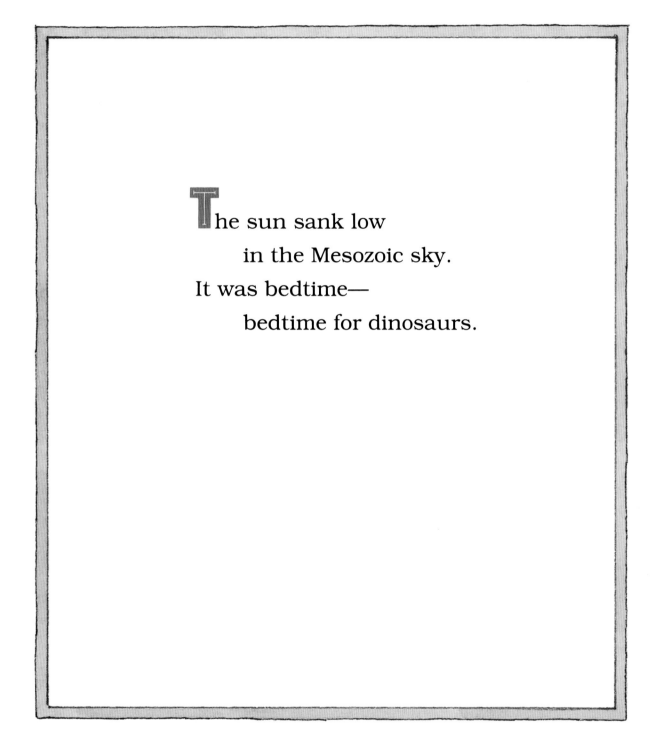

The sun sank low
    in the Mesozoic sky.
It was bedtime—
    bedtime for dinosaurs.

Tiny stegosauruses
Whispered creepy stories
Of the monsters in the forests
To trembling allosauruses.

Soon those scaredysauruses

Were snoring all in choruses

While snoozing

In the sweet

soft

ooze.

Good night, dinosaurs.

Sleep tight, dinosaurs.

Good night,

dinosaurs,

good night.

Two naughty young diplodocus
Screamed and made a dreadful fuss—

"We do not wish to brush our teeth!
To wash our necks would take a week!
We'd rather just play hide and seek."

Mom and Dad diplodocus
(Each one was bigger than a bus)
Chased them off to bed with hisses,
Followed by diplodokisses.

Good night, dinosaurs,
Don't fight, dinosaurs,
Good night,
     dinosaurs,
        good night.

Pteranodons
Put their nightgowns on.
There were bottles all around,

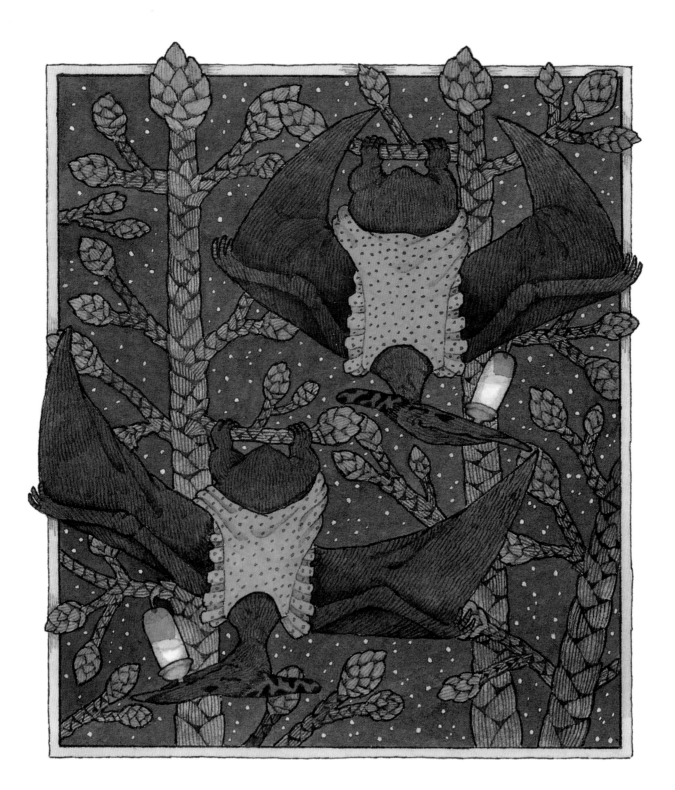

They were swinging upside down,
Forty feet above the ground,
Softly swaying to the sound
Of the dinosaurs' sleepytime song.

Good night, dinosaurs,
Hold on tight, dinosaurs,
Good night,
 dinosaurs,
  good night.

Three tyrannosaurus rexes
Once lay dreaming of their breakfasts
In what's now the state of Texas.

Then each fearsome future fossil
Yawned a yawn that was colossal;
As the moon lit up the sky,
And they nestled side by side,
Tyrannograndma sang that lizard lullaby.

Good night, dinosaurs,
Don't bite, dinosaurs,
Good night,
     dinosaurs,
        good night.

Just-hatched baby compsognathus,
With crinkly wrinkly baby faces,
Twitched their tails
And sucked their claws.
Amidst their family's "ooh's" and "aah's"
They opened up their tiny jaws,
Said their very first word,

peep

Closed their eyes,
       and fell asleep.

Rockabye, dinosaurs,
Don't cry, dinosaurs,
Good night,
       dinosaurs,
              good night.

Ten very tired triceratops
Sucked on seaweed lollipops
While sitting in a squishy fishy tub.
Their papa rubbed their scales,
And scrubbed their ticklish tails,
Until everybody yelled

PLEASE STOP!

Then they cuddled up together
By that prehistoric river
Till their eye-
                lids
                    dropped.

Good night, dinosaurs,
Shiny bright dinosaurs,
Good night,
        dinosaurs,
            good night.

And then Jupiter and Mars,
And a thousand shooting stars,
Sparkled in the night,
Sprinkling down their light
On that heap
        of sleeping reptiles
                in their

                Home Sweet Swamp.

Good night, dinosaurs,
Sleep tight, dinosaurs,
Good night,
    dinosaurs,
        good night.

MEET THE AUTHORS AND ILLUSTRATORS

Carol Carrick and Donald Carrick

CAROL CARRICK wrote many well-loved books for children, including *What Happened to Patrick's Dinosaurs?*, *Big Old Bones,* and *Patrick's Dinosaurs on the Internet.* Thirty-seven books were collaborations with her husband, Donald, and she created *Mothers Are Like That* with her son Paul, an artist and illustrator. She made her home on Martha's Vineyard.

DONALD CARRICK illustrated more than eighty books, many as collaborations with his wife, the author Carol Carrick. He shared the Christopher Award with Richard Margolis for *Secrets of a Small Brother,* illustrated *The Wednesday Surprise* by Eve Bunting, and was the author of several books, including *Morgan and the Artist.* Also a landscape painter, his subjects included locales from the Mediterranean to his family summer home in Vermont.

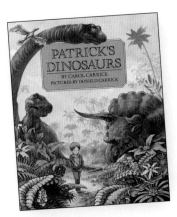

Margret and H. A. Rey

HANS AUGUSTO REY and MARGRET REY escaped Nazi-occupied Paris in 1940 by bicycle, carrying the manuscript for the first book about Curious George. They came to live in the United States, and *Curious George* was published in 1941. Since then, George has appeared in film, on television, and in many, many picture books about his adventures. He has been loved by millions of children all over the world for more than seventy years. You can learn more about the Reys and Curious George, and access games, activities, downloads, and episodes of the PBS television show at www.curiousgeorge.com.

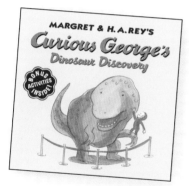
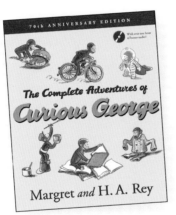

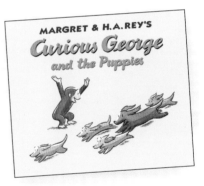

Bernard Most

BERNARD MOST has written and illustrated many popular children's books about dinosaurs and other animals, including *The Cow That Went OINK, Pets in Trumpets,* and *My Very Own Octopus.* He began writing dinosaur books for his son before becoming hooked on the creatures himself. Most, a father of two and grandfather of three, lives in Westchester, New York, with his wife, two cats named Bonnie and Clyde, and many tropical fish. Visit www.bernardmost.com to learn more.

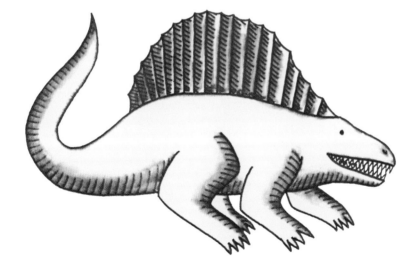

Kurt Cyrus

KURT CYRUS is a poet and writer and the illustrator of nearly twenty picture books, many of which he also wrote, including *Oddhopper Opera* and *Hotel Deep.* He had the idea for *Tadpole Rex* after finding frog eggs in his backyard pond. He lives near Eugene, Oregon. To learn more, visit www.kurtcyrus.com.

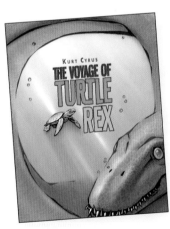

George McClements

GEORGE McCLEMENTS has been ridin' dinos since he was knee-high to a stegosaurus. He has written and illustrated several picture books, including *Night of the Veggie Monster, Dinosaur Woods,* and *The Last Badge.* After long days out on the range, he comes home to roost in Glendale, California, where he lives with his wife and their two young 'uns.

Julia Liu and Bei Lynn

JULIA LIU is the author of many children's picture books. Her work has been published in countries around the world, including China, South Korea, Brazil, and the United States. *Kirkus Reviews* called *Gus, the Dinosaur Bus* a "mix of Syd Hoff's *Danny and the Dinosaur* (1999) and Steven Kellogg's *The Mysterious Tadpole* (1997, 2002)." She lives in Taiwan.

BEI LYNN is an award-winning artist who has illustrated twenty picture books for children, some of which she has also written. Her illustrations are mainly made of watercolor and pencil and have been published in numerous magazines. Her first book, *To Be Fish,* was published in 1999, and the *China Times* has selected her books for its Best Children's Book of the Year list several times. She lives in Taiwan.

Deb Lund and Howard Fine

DEB LUND is a dino-fabulous picture book writer. In addition to her popular dino-transportation trilogy, she wrote *Monsters on Machines,* illustrated by Robert Neubecker. Deb is also a teacher, singer, unicycle rider, and mom to her three kids. She lives on an island in Washington. To learn more about Deb visit www.deblund.com.

HOWARD FINE was studying to become a dentist when he illustrated his first book, *Piggie Pie!.* Since then, he has illustrated many books, including *All Aboard the Dinotrain, A Piggie Christmas, Snoring Beauty,* and *Dinosauring.* He lives with his family in White Plains, New York. Visit his website at www.howardfineillustration.com to learn more.

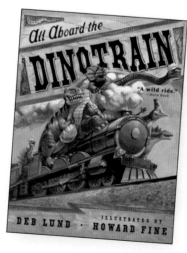

Judy Sierra and Victoria Chess

JUDY SIERRA holds a Ph.D. in folklore from UCLA. She is also the reteller/compiler of several books of folklore for teachers and storytellers. She was inspired to write picture books after hearing Uri Shulevitz state, "Picture books are small theaters." Since then, she has staged stories in many small theaters, including *Nursery Tales Around the World* and *Counting Crocodiles.* She lives in Oregon. Visit her website www.judysierra.net.

VICTORIA CHESS has illustrated more than one hundred books for children, including *Slugs* by David Greenberg, *Barbara Berman, Wedding Expert* by Jane Breskin Zalben, and *Fletcher and Zenobia* by Edward Gorey. She was born in Chicago, and studied at the Kokoshka School of Art in Salzburg, Austria, and the Museum of Fine Arts School in Boston. She lives in Massachusetts.

  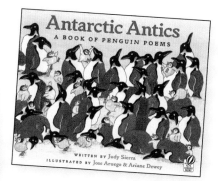 

Visit *www.hmhbooks.com/freedownloads* to download
and print accessories for your next dino party!

ACCESS CODE: GreatBigParty10072014

A HUGE thank-you!

_____

_____

_____

_____

You're invited to a roaring-good time!

WHAT _____

WHEN _____

WHERE _____

RSVP _____

INVITATIONS AND
THANK-YOU NOTES

BOOKMARK FAVORS

THIS IS MY FAVORITE **BOOK**, NO BONES ABOUT IT!

TAKE A **BITE** OUT OF BOOKS!

COLORING PAGES

BANNER FLAGS

IT'S A PARTY!

PLUS PUZZLES, GAMES, AND MORE!

THE END